This book would not have been possible without

the love, courage, and great company of our little

dog, Maloos.

Rescued!

Firouzeh Razavi

Rear and Roar

"You adopted a puppy?!" Melody exclaimed as she looked at her husband on the couch beside her. Martin awoke from a light drowse.

"What?" he asked dazedly. "What's going on?"

Melody pointed to the phone pressed up to her ear. *Bella adopted a puppy* she mouthed with great exaggeration.

"She did?!" he whispered gleefully. "That's great!"

"Yes, Mom," Bella's voice rang with excitement through the phone. "I've been thinking about it for years and when I saw that puppy I thought she was the most beautiful dog I'd ever seen! I put in an application to adopt her at the Pasadena Humane Society and they just called and told me I can pick her up!"

While happy for her daughter, Melody couldn't help but feel that it would have been better to wait a little longer. "That's very exciting, Bella," she began, "but don't you have your hands full with trying to find a full-time job? I'm worried you won't have time for a dog."

"No worries, Mom," Bella assured her. "I can manage it. I've been thinking about this and reading about what to expect for a long time. I know it's the right time…"

"I've told you," Melody interrupted, her voice echoing a familiar warning, "a puppy's love for you will grow fast and deep the second she enters your life. This budding love takes a lot of care. Abandoning this responsibility would be more than cruel, it would be crushing."

"Oh, I know, mom," Bella reassured. "Trust me, it's the right time, there's nothing to worry about." A slight pause did nothing to quell Melody's concerns. "You have to see her," Bella continued. "I will never find a dog as beautiful as her again."

"Maybe not," Melody said. Although her daughter's excitement was contagious, she hoped Bella would change her mind. "Well, are you sure you're going to be with that puppy for the rest of her life?" she asked grimly. "Because if you later change your mind, the puppy will forever think about you until the last day of her life."

"Mom!" Bella whined, annoyed at the sadness Melody kept injecting into the conversation. "That would never happen!"

Changing course, Melody asked, "So, when are you going to get her?"

"I'll be there tomorrow at 10am to pick her up," Bella said cheerfully. "You, Dad, and Grandma have to meet her; I can bring her to your favorite coffee shop after!"

"All right," Melody said hesitantly. "We'll be there."

"Great!"

Melody sighed. "Bye for now." She hung up, relaxing into her chair and tapping her fingertips together, as she usually did when anxious.

"How exciting!" Martin grinned. "When do we get to meet the puppy?"

"Tomorrow morning," Melody replied. "I hope this isn't a mistake. I tried to warn her, but she is determined."

"Don't say that," he shook his head. "She knows what she is doing. Besides, puppies are fun, no matter how much work they are."

Bella had always wanted a dog. However, because the condominiums she grew up in had "No Pet" policy, she never could fulfill that childhood dream. Both of her parents did, in fact, want their child to grow up with a pet to teach responsibility. Alas, living in a compact development with strict rules in the middle of a bustling city had made it impossible.

In 2010, Bella moved out of her parent's home to attend university forty miles away. There, she rented a small apartment. As a young woman she was a brilliant student, although a bit unhappy for having to leave her parent's home and the town she loved so much. It was there that the talk of getting a dog grew more frequent. Shortly after Bella settled in her apartment, Melody convinced her mother, Virginia, to move in with her and her husband. Virginia gladly accepted their offer.

Virginia had the wonder, enthusiasm, and excitement that little children have. Despite her age, she never grew old in spirit. She always exhibited kindness and thoughtfulness for others by putting their needs before her own. With just a smile, she could make you feel everything was all right and always would be. And she smiled a lot. Melody had tried to emulate her mother in almost every way and the respect that she had for her allowed them to enjoy each other's company. While Bella had adored Virginia, Melody worshiped her.

For nearly two years, Bella debated the same question aloud with herself and her family: *Should I get a dog?* Every occasion, every family get together, every phone call evolved into a spirited conversation over the life changing decision: Her father didn't want to stop her from fulfilling her dream. Her mother, on the other hand, implored her daughter to look past her wants and focus on responsibility. As considerately as possible, Melody always told her "The care of a puppy is very similar to the care of a child. It is not as easy as you think."

Determined to make sure Bella considered every aspect, Melody would repeatedly voice varied concerns: "If you need to travel or have an emergency, we can't bring your dog into our condo." "Consider the expenses: annual dog license, vet bills, training, grooming." "What if you become too busy?" "What if you have to relocate?"

For each point, Bella had an answer: "I can always kennel the dog at a pet hotel." "I can cut back on non-essential things to pay for the dog." "If I've to move, then the dog comes with me!" A few weeks after graduating from university, she finally decided to adopt a dog.

The Saturday morning after calling her parents, Bella drove to Pasadena. She was eager to adopt her dog, nervous for the impending shift in responsibility, and curious as to how the puppy would be received by her family. Melody waited on the coffee shop's patio with her husband and her mother, Virginia.

At around 10:30, Bella pulled into the parking lot. After a few minutes, she walked up to her family carrying a small bundle against her chest. "Everyone," she announced, a sheen of happy tears making her eyes glisten, "I want to introduce you to Maloos." Bella revealed a fluffy, apricot-colored, eight-week-old Maltipoo puppy.

Looking at the little puppy, Melody's worries vanished; she immediately fell in love with her. Watching her mother, Bella said, "I chose the name 'Maloos' not only because it means cute in Farsi, but because it is the name of the main character in your children's book."

Melody reached out and Bella carefully placed Maloos in her open hands. Overjoyed and holding Maloos's small, silky-haired body, Melody exclaimed with delight, "Oh, my little butterfly! I love you so much!" Shivering, the puppy looked at Melody with big, curious eyes. Melody gently brushed hair from her bright, hazelnut eyes, and said to her mother, "Oh, boy! Isn't this the cutest puppy you've ever seen?"

Virginia looked at the puppy and said, without much enthusiasm, "Yes, she is very beautiful, a heart-stealer for sure. But she will require *a lot* of care and attention."

Melody cut her off and said, "Well, I'm sure Maloos will make fine companion for Bella."

"Yeah," Virginia nodded, "she will make a smart and affectionate pet. But still, she *does* require much attention and care." She paused and looked at Maloos, her wide eyes staring back at her, curiously examining the oldest member of her new pack. "No doubt she will soon be one of our cherished family members," she said with a smile.

As everyone cooed over the little pup, it was clear that Maloos pulled at their heartstrings. Before Maloos had even been taken home, she had won everyone's affection, becoming the newest member of the family.

In the beginning, Bella didn't know much about raising a puppy. For months she focused on Maloos's look. Powdered, perfumed, and beribboned, Maloos accepted the dotage with courtly dignity. Month after month, coifed from the hairdresser came Maloos, a little dog with big appeal.

Bella eventually learned to raise Maloos by researching training techniques, and by trial and error. Maloos, fortunately, was quick to learn, but loved to challenge the rules, often developing ways to sidestep commands of "Leave it," "Come here," and "Drop it". Bella, sincerely trying her best, understood when she hit a wall in progress and sought the advice of a dog trainer.

Maloos's strong, compact frame, intelligent expression, and the color and texture of her coat made her look like a poodle in miniature. Her personality, however, was uniquely her own: Maloos loved to be surrounded by people, no matter what they were doing. She was intelligent, curious, and afraid of little. She was sweet, gentle, and completely stubborn. Her alert mind, coupled with the inherently playful nature of the Maltipoo breed, made her a sensible, dependable family dog.

As time passed, Melody's interest in Maloos grew and she learned more about her. Melody noticed that when her old mother held Maloos to her stomach or lap, the aches and pains she constantly felt went away. Placing her at the feet of her mother offered a sure cure for her severe rheumatism and arthritis.

Every time Melody and Martin visited Bella's home, Maloos would crane her neck to see them walk through the door. She would jump up and down, whining with excited impatience to make physical contact with them. When she reached them, her tail would wag so forcefully her whole body would shake. She would twist in-between their legs, getting tangled up. If they ignored her, she would then stand up, front legs stretched out, and jump up and down as if to say, *Look at me!*

Maloos, ever the center of attention, would become angry if Bella or her boyfriend, Jeff, paid too much attention to another dog: her jealousy would start as a low grumble in her throat as she stared. The grumble would turn into a series of high-pitched barks. She would side eye her owners as if to warn them against giving away any more precious attention. Bella and Jeff learned that Maloos relied heavily upon her pack in the outside world: she needed to know where they were at all times. Often, dog trainers found Bella was the problem: her doting, smothering, and attachment resulted in Maloos's complete dependence. When Bella ceased the unhealthy actions, Maloos became a more independent member of the family, learning to stifle her instinctual jealousy.

Maloos could even distinguish between the sound of Bella or Jeff's car from others of the same make. Her internal clock was so tuned that she could predict when they would return home from work and would sit patiently waiting for them to walk through the door. She also knew that Saturdays and Sundays meant no work and was eager to start the day with an exploratory romp outside.

Birds of a Feather

Maloos loved to wear clothes because of the attention it got her. She had a lavish wardrobe consisting of dresses, pajamas, cashmere sweaters, snowsuits, rhinestone collars, jeweled berets, toenail polish, even a small plated California license with her name and address written on it. After being dressed, she would run to each person in the house to show off her new garb. Bella even taught her to wear plastic booties to protect her groomed feet against the wet snow when they visited the family cabin in the mountains. Struggling into and out of form-fitting jackets and strutting on the street at least provided some of the exercise she needed. When out, Maloos would scan the crowds and drive forward with laser focus to those who noticed her, desperate to say hello and receive some love in return.

Maloos would seldom walk far. She wasn't interested in treading the same path more than once: She would sit, her front legs stretched out in protest, the leash taut as Bella tried to coax her forward a few more steps. Instead, Maloos loved new places, new sights, and new smells. When they visited the family cabin, however, she enjoyed walking in the village, peering into the stores, and watching the crowds and the busy streets. Being able to experience changing seasons granted Maloos's desire to investigate new sceneries and more than likely contributed to her boredom in the mundane city in which she lived.

As time passed, the bond between Melody and Maloos grew stronger. She learned that Maloos liked to be with people and to do what they were doing. She learned that Maloos wasn't particularly patient with children, attempting to scold loud or running children with sharp, percussive barks. Mostly, Melody learned that Maloos loved the mountains as much as she did.

The steep, rocky hillsides, the endlessly expansive forest, and the various lakes peppered up and down the slopes were a sanctuary inside Melody's mind: Winter sees the landscape blanketed as the flora, fauna, and animal life hibernate. Spring sheds the snow, causing life to rise anew. Summer brings more life as crowds swarm lakes and cabins to relax, fish, cook, and party with friends and family. In the fall, everything begins to slow down as leaves begin to blush, painting the landscape with an array of vibrant reds, yellows, and oranges.

Stuck in the cabin through her first winter as she finished her shots, Maloos would stare at the snow-covered ground and trees from the couch under the window in the living room. She would longingly scan the landscape, anxious to explore whatever wonder lay outside. When she was carried out to the car, she would crane her head, her nose searching the air to identify and detect the smell of fire burning in fireplaces or the pungent scent of pine mixed with fresh snow.

While the cabin brought comfort, warmth, and the presence of loved ones, Maloos faced a daunting obstacle: the stairs. Melody, determined to have Maloos exercise her bravery, left her on one floor and went to the next. After a few minutes, Maloos overcame her fear: she cautiously climbed up every step. She then explored the unchartered territory by roaming and sniffing through each room. Melody knew most puppies were afraid of stairs but believed that Maloos's courage would help master them in no time.

Indeed, Maloos relinquished her fear of going up the steep steps, eventually running up them at lightning speed. Coming down, however, was the next challenge: she would sit at the top of the stairs, helplessly barking her tiny puppy bark. It became a game for the humans: Maloos would chase them up the stairs, circling through the bedrooms and then come to a halt, watching them run back down laughing with glee as she barked from the top.

Melody decided that enough fun had been had at Maloos's expense and began teaching her to come down independently. She kneeled on the steps, face to face with Maloos. Placing a small treat on the step below and on the opposite side of Maloos, she coaxed her down. Maloos kept two paws on the higher step, two on the lower and gobbled the treat. Melody then put another treat on the opposite end, one step lower. She repeated this, luring Maloos down the stairs. Melody then ran back up the stairs, Maloos following right behind, and coaxed her down again. They did this a handful of times until Maloos gained the confidence to come down herself. However, because Melody had put the treats on the opposite ends of the stairs, Maloos would zigzag down the stairs. Everybody laughed as Melody showed them how Maloos finally learned to come descend.

Melody and Maloos became inseparable while in the mountains together. They would drive around the lake, leisurely taking in the wonders; the crystal refraction of waves bouncing off the sunlight; the soaring bald eagles; the animals scuttering and bounding through thickets of trees and brush.

One rainy spring day, as Melody was driving around the lake, Maloos took her usual position of copilot beside her, her paws on the door's armrest, her breath fogging the window as she stared out. Melody decided to put on one of her favorite songs. As the cabin filled with the sound of music, Maloos turned to look at Melody. She then laid down in her seat and stared up at the rain pouring down over the car windows. When the song ended, Maloos stood up, looked at Melody, and barked. Melody told her to sit down. Maloos obeyed but kept barking. Melody played the song once again and Maloos quieted. She laid down again and listened delightedly as if she appreciated every note, every beat, every lyric. From that day on, Melody always kept Maloos's song ready for their next adventure around the lake.

Maloos loved being in the mountains more than any other place. She never tired of walking the trails, driving around the lake, strutting on the boardwalk, or people-watching in the village. She was ready to go at any time. When she knew they were going, she would wag her entire small body. Most of all, she enjoyed the swings and slides and merry-go-round in the park playground just like a kid. When it was time to leave, she planted herself, her front legs spread out as she sat forcefully on the ground. She would stare into the eyes of whomever held the leash, as if daring them to make her move.

After a long weekend in the mountains, Maloos's curly, strawberry blonde coat would be matted, dusty, and tangled with twigs. The weekend mountaineer would need a bath to become civilized once more. "Maloos," Melody would ask, pausing dramatically between each word, "do you want to take a shower?" Maloos's head would twist from side to side as she listened, her eyes locked on Melody's. Upon hearing the word "shower," her eyes would widen and she would dart upstairs, jump into the bathtub, and sit waiting for Melody to follow. Maloos offered up her paws as the water poured down and Melody's fingers lathered her coat with coconut scented shampoo. She spun around when it was time to wash her hindquarters and sat patiently as dirt and grime were picked from her eyes and ears. She then let Melody blow-dry her coat into her unique, perfectly bouncy style.

Dog Days

Maloos loved Thanksgiving and Christmas as everyone was brought together under the cabin roof. That time of year was carved out for family time in the cabin, no matter what. Bella, Jeff, and Maloos would travel up the mountain from Orange County. Virginia, Melody, and Martin drove from Los Angeles. The growing chill in the air meant that Maloos would don sweaters, coats, and thick pajamas during her visit. The cabin was filled with the aroma of nonstop cooking: turkey, ham, biscuits, cookies, cakes, casseroles, and smashed, mashed, sautéed, and roasted veggies tortured Maloos to no end. She would watch Melody prepare every meal, her eyes fixated on her favorite show: The Cooking Show. The second the refrigerator door opened, Maloos would run over and sit just outside of the kitchen. Her eyes transfixed, she watched every slice, dice, stir, measure, and pour. She would crane her neck, her nose taking in the aromas of whatever was on the stove. Her head constantly rotated as ingredients were added to simmering pans and pots. Most of all, she loved getting samples: cheese, lettuce, chips, broccoli, and sweet peppers always found their way into her salivating mouth. Carrots and banana were left on the floor, spit out and rejected. When it came time to clean up, however, Maloos would vanish. Bella joked that if Maloos were human, she would be the greatest chef the world had ever seen, but her kitchen would be a disaster.

Cooking was a labor of love for Melody; her daily existence was inextricably entwined with family. Crafting her signature dishes and flavors was how she showed love and appreciation. She enjoyed getting out the fine china and setting the table with scented candles, shiny gold tablecloths and colorful runners, and enough silver utensils to cause argyria. She strived to make every meal a feast that would be remembered for years, even after she left this world. Her joy was sitting at the table, basking in the love and friendship. She happily scanned the faces of her family as they counted their blessings and partook of her food.

No other day was so exciting as Christmas Eve. Maloos would lay with her family in front of the fireplace as they laughed and played games. Pine logs crackled and burned brightly in the fireplace as a huge ham roasted in the oven. Gifts piled atop each other, tempting impatient eyes who were jokingly called out for being just so. Christmas music played softly as lights from a tinsel-strewn tree danced along. With all the lights off except those on the tree, the living room seemed magical. After dinner, Melody handed out the gifts. Stacks of metallic wrapped boxes created a fortress around each person. As they tore into the gifts, shouts of glee echoed through the cabin. Each gift was held up and cherished: Electronics, clothes, candies and chocolates, the practical and not-so-much.

Maloos, filled with fervor and excitement, would run through the maze of torn wrappings and discarded boxes, snatching up and shredding as much as possible before it was taken away. She soon learned that Christmas brought new toys for her, too: balls, squeaky toys, ropes, and frisbees. She scratched through wrapping paper to get her prize and would carry it under the table to examine it before being distracted by another.

After all the gifts were tucked away and the living room was cleaned, the humans played Hide-and-Seek with Maloos: Melody and Bella would hide upstairs and call out "Maloos! Come find me!" She would run up the stairs and jump on the bed, sniffing out any bump she thought could be them. She nudged open doors, peered under beds, and sniffed through closets. When she eventually found them, she would wag her tail and bark. The found party would then run downstairs.

Then it was Maloos's turn to hide. As good a hunter as she was, she couldn't hide to save her life: Maloos would put her head behind some pillows, under a comforter, or under the bed so she couldn't see. However, her legs, torso, and wagging tail would be sticking out. They would pretend to look for her, calling out "Maloos, where are you?" until one of them yelled "Gotcha!" and Maloos would run out of the room and zigzag down the stairs. On and on this went until they couldn't make it up the stairs anymore.

All the scraps and half-eaten bits of food collected in trash bags eventually gained the attention of racoons. These creatures, deemed mortal enemies by Maloos, caused her great anxiety. The slightest scamper across the roof, the faintest sound of a trashcan lid coming off, the quietest crinkle of a torn trash bag, was enough to set Maloos on a barking spree throughout the cabin at any hour of night. The bandits would then flee and Maloos would return triumphantly to her warm spot on the bed.

The first snowfall of the season brought much excitement. Maloos loved to watch snow fall gingerly down to the ground from her cherished spot on the couch under the large living room window. She attempted to examine each flake, her eyes darting up and down, left and right, before it crashed into the ever-growing quilt of fluff below. Most of all, Maloos couldn't wait to play in the snow. She would run around, kicking up powder in explosive gusts. She would then bury her face in the fresh powder. Lifting her face, she showed off her white beard to the great amusement of her family. Everyone struggled to keep up with her as she ran and jumped through the snow, leaping like a miniature, furry gazelle. She enjoyed sledding down their steep street, then coming home, eating treats, and lying down on her warm pillow on the couch under the window. For Melody, there was nothing more joyous than laying down on the couch under the living room window and looking out at the blue sky with her faithful dog there to keep her company.

As time passed, everyone developed a special bond with Maloos: Bella and Maloos napped together, cuddling under a warm blanket; Martin and Maloos explored together, visiting their favorite spots and picking up treats of fries and cookies along the way; Jeff and Maloos played together, tugging and chasing toys throughout the house and yard; Melody and Maloos relaxed together with Melody reading her books aloud to Maloos as they sat in the cabin's warm comfort.

****

In the summer of 2016, Bella, Jeff, and Maloos moved into their new home. Melody was happier than ever for them; they had more room to run around, play, and grow together. In time, they learned that Maloos had a special way of communicating with them: She looked them in eyes and barked softly when she wanted something like food or ice in her water. She taught herself to sit by the door and hit it to signal that she needed to go potty. She learned to bring them to the cupboard when she wanted a treat. She understood when she needed to be quiet, like at night when the frogs would croak just outside the bedroom window. She knew when she could have free reign of the house and when she needed to be confined to the downstairs. As all the new traits began to show, Bella would call her mom to boast about Maloos's extreme intelligence: "Mom," she would start, a hint of astonishment in her voice, "you won't believe what Maloos just did…" Melody took pride in the fact that her daughter and the little family she was starting were so happy in their discovery of everything new about each other.

During every visit to Bella's house, Maloos brought Melody or Virginia or Martin a toy out of her overflowing toy box that she wanted to play with. It had to be that toy in particular, otherwise, she would turn away.

Life was going happily and smoothly for all of them until October 2017, when Virginia became sick after a trip to the mountains. She was diagnosed with pneumonia, the x-ray of her lungs showed clusters of white spots. Virginia was given antibiotics and told to rest. It seemed as if recovery was just around the corner. One Saturday, however, there was a sudden change in the weather. Virginia's symptoms returned with a vengeance: she had a persistent cough, deep pain in her chest, and increased difficulty breathing. Melody rushed her to the hospital where Virginia was given oxygen, medication, and an IV. On Monday evening all hope was abandoned by her doctor, who informed Melody that her mother's health was declining fast.

Virginia's family found it hard to believe: She was alert and responsive, albeit tired and unable to speak. Early Wednesday morning found her less mobile, though still aware she was in the hospital. With Melody's help, Virginia sat up in bed while her daughter combed her hair. She seemed so tranquil that Melody and her family decided to let her rest for an hour or two while they went to get dinner. They had been away about an hour when Melody's telephone rang. Virginia's doctor was on the other end of the line and said, "I think you should return to hospital as soon as you can."

"Is my mom ok?" Melody asked fearfully.

The doctor's tone grew grim as he said, "Your mom's condition is looking bleak. She has been struggling to breathe for the last hour."

Melody inhaled sharply and said, "We'll be there shortly."

All eyes were on Melody as she hung up the phone. The diner they sat in seemed to grow quiet. Melody, gathering her things from the table, said, "That was mom's doctor." She held back tears and avoided making eye contact with anyone. "He said that her condition is worsening and that we should all get to the hospital."

"Good God let's go!" Martin said.

There was a flurry of activity as everyone stood up. Jeff stayed back to settle their tab while everyone else ran to their cars.

Melody's mind began wandering as Martin accelerated out of the parking lot. Martin pulled onto the on-ramp of the 210 West freeway and accelerated towards Huntington Hospital.

As Martin drove, visions of Melody's past overtook her: the first day her mother took her to school, the look of pride on her mother's face at her graduation, Thanksgivings, Christmases, all hosted with love and joy at her table. When she, her brothers, and sister came home from school on snowy afternoons, they got to sample hot apple butter on fresh homemade bread. The memories came and went so fast as Martin pulled into Huntington hospital's parking lot. It was dark outside. The light from hospital lobby was pouring out of the big glass windows. Not much activity was inside the lobby. They rushed past the receptionist while pointing to their visitor stickers. They rode the elevator up to the fifth floor and hurried quietly down the hall. The whole floor was quiet, as if a shroud of silence had befallen its residents. Melody couldn't hold back her tears and dabbed her eyes with a wad of Kleenex.

They finally arrived at room 500 and Melody saw that they were the last ones to arrive. A nurse with a clipboard was just finishing her visit. Before the nurse could relay any information, her sister came rushing across room and gave her a big hug. Melody put her arms around her sister. They cried quietly. She then walked over to the bed where her mother was lying surrounded by her two brothers and sisters-in-law. Her pale face was swollen. She bent and kissed her forehead a few times, and whispered, "I love you, Mom."

Virginia smiled frailly at Melody and, her voice hoarse, said, "I love you more." She looked dazed as her eyes weakly took in her daughter's face.

There, surrounded by family, feebly gazing up from her bed, she inhaled one deep breath, closed her eyes and died.

Virginia left them with only memories of her long, last journey. A few hours later, they all left the hospital with their red, watery eyes swollen from tears.

After her mother's funeral, Melody felt a strange kind of loneliness. She knew in her heart it would be a long while before she was able to get over the loss. Some nights, as she laid in bed, she thought she heard the distant sound of her mother's voice. She felt as if her soul had disintegrated inside of her, leaving a hollow, broken shell. Deep grief caused her to stagger and slump into depression.

With this quandary, her creative outlets felt cut off; she couldn't finish writing the new manuscript that she'd been working on for so long. Her interest in painting and writing were gone. She believed in strength but had lost hers. Eventually, with no creativity left, and no desire to search for it, she felt like she had stopped living.

Then her health quit. She was taken to the hospital, suffering from severe pneumonia and later a complete mental and physical breakdown. To her, physical, mental, and spiritual decay were all tied together.

Every day, she was yearning for her mother, looking for her in her room, poring over picture albums and talking about her all the time, almost as if she were there, somehow physically prolonging Melody's grief. She couldn't stand the pain. Nothing felt pleasurable. She didn't have any ordinary grief, she had persistence grief in her brain that didn't go away.

From the beginning, her husband and daughter recognized the special challenge of grief and its relationship to her depression.

One day, as Melody and Martin were sitting at the dining room table sipping coffee, Melody grew quiet and stared off. Martin asked if anything was wrong. Turning toward him on the verge of tears, she sobbed, "You'll never know how much I miss my mom." He put his arm around her, pulled her close. Giving her a warm kiss, he whispered in her ear, "I know. I know." Melody erupted into tears. She didn't have the words.

Weeks came and went, and Melody's emotions piled upon themselves. Crippled by an inability to forget and move on, her spirit felt underground and undernourished. Questions of life and mortality filled her psyche until it felt as if her spirit was kicking her brain out of her body. For weeks, Melody wrote nothing, painted nothing. She cooked nothing and could barely eat.

Bella was very worried and voiced her concerns: "You need to eat and get some rest, Mom," she pleaded. "You can't keep this up."

Melody just looked at Bella, her eyes beseeching. "We all wish to press on," Melody replied cryptically, "to outgrow our present limitations. I want to move on, but how can I? I keep reliving that day when my mother passed away in front of my eyes."

"You are the master of your own life," Bella replied, "not some leaf in a whirlwind of fate. You can do it. I know you can. We have to accept this reality eventually, even though it's nothing any of us want."

Melody realized the persistence of her grief had interfered with her daily functioning and worse than that had stopped her inspiration of art. She had dragged on for weeks, living mechanically, indifferent to what became of her. Depression was sapping life from her.

One way or another, she thought, *I will have to deal with my emotions.* Thinking she couldn't live fully in the present, she decided to place distance between herself and the grief that was robbing her of peace. Weeks passed in blurred agony. She tried forcing herself to resume a normal routine. One day, she thought about going to the family cabin for respite. She was soon resolute in her decision to go; to look the world in the face and ponder her future. She told her family that she would go to their cabin alone for a few days to clear her mind. After all, the mountains were her sacred space; a natural sanctuary just right for contemplating the deep questions about life and mortality. Her solitude there had helped her find herself again and again.

She explained to her husband and daughter that she was having a hard time handling her feelings. She explained how she cried so many nights, that she was falling behind on projects, that she didn't know how to help herself. She explained how going to the mountains could help make peace with the life without her beloved mother.

She thought they might argue, but they didn't. Going to the mountains, they thought, was the smart thing to do; staying in their cabin was good for her and would give her a chance to resolve at least some of her emotions.

However, Bella was alarmed about her mother's deep grieving and pleaded to join her. Melody, determined to spend time alone, declined.

Knowing that her mother's resolve was unmovable, Bella suggested that Maloos's presence could be therapeutic. "If you won't let me come," Bella said, "then at least take Maloos."

"I really don't want the added responsibility," Melody resisted.

"Responsibility?" Bella protested. "Maloos is all comfort and entertainment!" Bella insisted. "Please, *please* take her with you."

Though the pain in her heart wanted solitude, Melody knew that Bella wouldn't relent. "All right," she finally conceded. "I'll take Maloos. But if she turns out to be too much, I will bring her back."

Bella breathed a sigh of relief. "Thank you, Mom! Maloos will be so excited."

Sirius Navigating

One cold Monday morning in February 2018, Melody gathered her things. She then made her way to her daughter's home. With great reluctance, Melody drove to get Maloos. Arriving around 9 a.m., she found Bella and Maloos coming out to greet her. Maloos knew that she was in for an adventure: Her packed food and clothing meant a mountain trip was in store. Maloos greeted Melody with her happy wagging tail and excitement brimming in her eyes.

"Hi, Mom!" Bella called as Melody got out of her car. Melody hid her unwillingness to take Maloos on her trip.

Bella gave her a big hug as Maloos jumped up and down excitedly. "You're looking better today," Bella remarked. "Most of the time you look sad and tired, almost as if you're sick."

"Gee, thanks," Melody responded. But she got it. For Bella, it was hard to imagine her rock of strength crumbling so. Bella looked at her mother. Melody assured her daughter that she was fine, but Bella looked skeptical. Regardless, she began buckling Maloos into the passenger seat. She then handed Melody a cup of hot chocolate, a lunch bag filled with snacks and a sandwich, and a new toy for Maloos.

"Try not to think too much about Grandma," she said. "We can't do anything to change what happened. Try to give yourself some time. Have fun with Maloos. Give her the new toy when you're sad, and it'll brighten both your moods."

With a kind smile, Melody replied, "Ok, I will."

Bella gave her a long, warm hug, then wished them a safe trip. Off went Melody and Maloos, the two of them determined to quit civilization and make their way to the mountains in search of peace.

Maloos stood on the seat, front paws on the window ledge, looking back at Bella as the distance grew between them. Melody expected her to whine or panic, but Maloos just turned her head then watched whatever dogs watch when they stare out a car window.

Maloos lived in the present and focused on her comfort, no matter where she went or what was coming. She entertained herself by barking at passersby until the window was sealed as they accessed the freeway. Thankfully, there was little traffic.

Eventually, Melody left the freeway and accessed the foothills. Even so, despite the companion beside her, she felt anything but jubilant. Rain and fog seemed to conspire to occlude the mountains' shoulders. She could barely see the road ahead. As dense as it was, the fog instantaneously lifted, revealing a clear, breathtaking view of house-sized, grey boulders, conifers and oaks and buckthorn-strewn, steep slopes. Melody pulled off to absorb the grandeur. Maloos brimmed with the anticipation of adventure. They continued ascending Highway 18.

At Lakeview Point, crisp blue waters unfurled before them, reminding those who made the trek that the destination is worth the journey. Melody and Maloos left the car then stood in silence and awe at the lookout, trying to accomplish the impossible by taking *everything* in. As she drank the last of her hot chocolate, Melody recalled coming home from school: Her mother would sometimes have a steamy mug of hot chocolate made in a pan with milk and cocoa and sugar, not from a packet of dry mix, waiting for her. Sugar-invigorated, she would then play outside in the snow for hours and return to a warm house where her mom would help peel off wet clothes crusted with chunks of ice.

For a moment, Melody felt as if she were free-falling down the mountain side, disappearing into the dark fog between the seemingly endless divide.

What is the point of going to a mountain retreat where memories of a life now dead plague the living? She had lost her father a few years ago, but this grief was not the same.

With a sigh, she and Maloos got back into the car and resumed their leisurely ascent. Maloos stuck her head out of the window, enjoying the cold, fresh air. *To be so carefree and unaware,* Melody thought, the conclusion evading her. She took a few deep breaths then began talking to Maloos as if sharing thoughts with a friend. She told her all about her mother's death. She cried. With tears streaming she said, "Oh, Maloos, if you could only know how badly I hurt! If only you could know…" she looked down at Maloos, struck speechless by the expression on Maloos's face.

Maloos understood what a quivering voice meant. Sensitive to moods, she knew something was very wrong. She responded to Melody's tears by dropping her ears, widening her eyes, and trying to get closer to her. It was as if she was saying, "What's happening here? What's wrong? Why are you crying?" She put a paw on Melody's lap and tried to nuzzle her. Melody took a few deep breaths and sobbed.

Maloos cocked her eyes at her with a look of curious wonder. Her paws once again laid lightly on Melody's lap, she tried again to nuzzle her. Maloos, through her love, was speaking in ways that were perfect and unfailing.

Melody glanced down at Maloos, tears on her eyelashes, her lips quivering, and told her, "Maloos, you are a precious creature. You *understand*!" Wiping her tears, she continued talking to her, so the sadness didn't stay as a lump in her stomach.

"I'm very sad," she said, sobbing, "I'm deeply hurt."

Describing the situation to Maloos helped her decode what she was feeling and helped her see how to let go. Maloos was so in tune that Melody forgot she was a dog. Being able to speak the way she needed to, to an unbiased, perfectly innocent creature, liberated her. To not be told the same old clichés somehow worked. She felt her heart swell with love as Maloos simply gazed at her, cocking and twisting her head as a dog does when trying to understand complex, silly humans.

"Oh, Maloos!" she stroked her head affectionately, "I don't know what to do with my grief!" she paused and wiped her tears.

Maloos sat back and growled softly, eyeing Melody as if to say: "Hang in! Lifting up! Time resolve not immediate! Believe or not, if stick hope, you celebrate life, not less! Don't let sorrow goes higher than knees! Stick hope! Bark like stranger might good! Like stairs!"

Melody knew that she was projecting; who knows what goes on in a dog's mind? For all she knew, Maloos could have wanted her to be quiet. However, believing that Maloos cared about her and wanted her to feel better helped lighten her load.

****

They reached Cabin shortly after 11. Melody got out of the car. The crisp mountain air swirled; trees whipped in the wind. Telling Maloos to wait, she closed the car door. Maloos whimpered. Melody took her bags from the trunk then carried them in. She immediately opened the curtains. Light flooded in, bringing life to the home. Wind and rain had knocked all the leaves off their backyard aspen trees. The cabin, unoccupied for months, was freezing. The furnace roared as she cranked the heater to 78 degrees. She exited the cabin, returning to the car to find Maloos sitting alert and watchful, as if saying, "Get me out!"

Opening the car door, she grabbed the leash and unbuckled Maloos from her restraints. Maloos excitedly jumped out of the car and pulled Melody into the house. The cabin was still cold as she closed the door behind them. She unleashed Maloos and let her roam. She ran upstairs and fetched one of her favorite toys. Melody took the bags upstairs to the master bedroom, then filled Maloos' dishes: one with dog food, the other with water. Maloos, hungry as a bear, slurped, crunched, and swallowed happily. Melody felt a twinge of hunger but couldn't bring herself to eat. Maloos then jumped onto her spot on the couch, a ray of sunlight beaming down on her, and promptly fell asleep. Melody sat on the same couch, picked up a nearby magazine, and read.

Maloos awoke an hour later and sat by the front door, indicating that she had to relieve herself. Melody bundled up, put a little red coat on Maloos, leashed her, and they went out. The cold air outside surprised Melody, making her inhale sharply as they walked up the street, her sadness expanding all around her. The street was quiet, as the midweek usually was in the mountains. A dark cloud blew in, casting a grey gloom over the mountain top. She loved the sudden change in weather but felt that she had to try to change her mood in order to enjoy her surroundings. She took Maloos to her favorite pathway by the lake for a little while, even though it was cloudy and cold.

As they walked up the steep hill alongside their house, Maloos found a stick. She picked up the stick in her mouth and happily went on. The deserted neighborhood was eerie yet comforting as they walked the path in solitude, the distraction of cars, bicyclists, and fellow pedestrians proving pleasantly absent. The aromatic scent of pine filled the air. She saw visions of her family walking the same path and wished she could fly away to another time, another reality where they stayed on the same happy, united path she had envisioned.

Reaching the top of the hill, they saw a middle-aged couple holding hands and walking. Maloos pulled Melody closer to the strangers, her tail wagging, the stick falling from her mouth, forgotten as something more important took her attention. The couple stopped to say hello and patted Maloos lovingly. They warned Melody that coyotes had been spotted in the area several times, and that they were running in packs. They also warned her not to go far: "The weather could change abruptly," the man said.

"That's true, thank you for telling me. We won't go far," she said as they parted ways. Melody preferred not to think about possible dangers just then; the two continued walking down the hill.

Down the hill, Melody caught sight of the magnificent lake: the serene imagery of trees, water, boulders, and wildlife existed unmarred by urban development. As she stood in awe before the lovely scene, the soothing atmosphere physically enveloped her and lifted her soul above its daily problems.

She raised her face to the dark, cloudy sky. She silenced her mind and listened to the wind. She felt calm and remembered that she saw an eagle the last time she stood in that very spot. She recalled her youth when she would sit in a willow tree in the front yard of her childhood home and sing at the top of her lungs accompanied by the howling voice of her childhood dog, Bumbooli.

Melody and Maloos continued. Crossing the road took her to the boardwalk, Maloos's favorite pathway. They walked to the end of the long boardwalk and sat on a weathered wood bench looking out at a scene straight from a painting. She and Maloos were silent as they sat and stared at the lake and the mountains, a chilled breeze blowing softly on their face.

The still water reflected the landscape surrounding it, giving the illusion that the world was both upside-down and right-side up at the same time. "Mirror, mirror," she murmured to herself, completing her incantation in silence.

The lake swirled, deep greens and brilliant blues chasing earthy tones and cottony whites until the whirlpool revealed snapshots of Thanksgivings, Christmases, and summers spent in the mountains with her family. Visions of turkey feasts being prepared played on the lake, the whole family laughing as Virginia exaggeratedly removed innards and stuffed the bird. The image blurred. Then bows were flying and paper was strewn all over the living room as they opened presents. The image blurred and came into focus again: they were gathered around the fireplace drinking eggnog. Then they were outside sneaking peaks at the feast cooking on the barbeque and chasing Maloos all around the yard. Then they were sitting on the deck in the backyard, watching fireworks explode above.

The fireworks faded, the sky remained dark. The image made the center of her chest feel hollow and dull.

The emptiness caused her to wince. When she opened her eyes, the lake was reflecting its surroundings once again.

She did her best to stay still, but what she really wanted to do was twirl and leap and shout out the wonder and anger and sadness that coursed through her veins. Maloos sat beside her, her gaze transfixed on some unseen intrigue in the water, her tiny body statuesque.

Tears leaked down Melody's face as she gazed into the lake's reflection. She sat still for what seemed an eternity. Finally, a stiff breeze told her it was time to go.

As they walked the boardwalk, a circling shadow on the ground drew Melody's gaze upward. She stopped. "Maloos," she said, and pointed up the sky at a vulture circling an animal that had met its demise. Maloos looked up towards, then past, the pointed finger, her eyes following the sprawling wings as they spun slowly.

The wind became stronger, colder. Dark clouds flew in, blotting out the vulture's shadow. The pair picked up the pace as snow began to fall, the first snow of the

season. Both shared a love for snow: Maloos enjoyed the

touch of snow on her eyelashes and opened her mouth to

grab snowflakes as they fell. She loved playing in the snow,

often bowing playfully as if to say, "Oh yeah, I can take

you if I really want to!" She would then run in dizzying

circles as fast as she could until she got tired. Ever the

showoff, she couldn't help displaying her prowess, circling

round and round until Melody was dizzy. They pursued

each other in the falling snow. Maloos barked playfully,

grunting as she chased and was chased. Melody couldn't

stop laughing at the pure energy and joy Maloos was

exuding. Maloos looked funny in her oversized red coat, its

hood slipping down over her eyes. Melody scooped up a

handful of fresh snow and tossed it playfully at Maloos.

Maloos bit at it as white dust covered her face.

Big, dark clouds sailed by with the eerie sound of

the wind. Not long after, the snowstorm descended with a

roar. Maloos enjoyed the crisp winter air, still wanting to play in the downpour. Melody shivered and said, "Perhaps we should go home now." Maloos looked at her and barked, as if saying, "Can't we play a little more?" Melody looked at Maloos with a smile that hadn't crossed her face in a long time and obliged. She recalled when Maloos jumped into snow for the first time, discovering the icy substance with glee.

Finally, they headed back toward the cabin. She tugged her hat down over her ears, covered her neck with her scarf and kept walking. The route was steep and slick. Maloos, now cold, seemed suddenly eager to get home quickly. At one point, she sat, refusing to walk any further. Her legs were trembling, her heart thumping wildly. Melody picked her up, wrapped her in her coat, held her close to her chest, and hurriedly carried her home.

The pine trees, carrying the weight of winter's first snowfall, were more beautiful than ever. Brown branches poked out from a growing blanket of white as Melody passed shrubs and bushes. The cabin might as well have been a distant planet. Her feet felt as if they were frozen solid and she could hardly wait to get to home. Her hands clutched Maloos closer to her chest, providing some warmth to both of them. Her face burned like fire and tears ran down her cheeks as she blinked against the cold wind.

Each step became more difficult: the thin mountain air seemed sparse, causing Melody to take short, shallow breaths. Maloos began to feel heavier. Both shivered as they walked against the cold wind and sleet. "You can never trust the weather in the mountains," she said, gripping Maloos tighter.

The welcome sight of the cabin appeared a short distance ahead just as Maloos let out sigh, as if to say, "Are we there yet?"

Canis Major

They reached home a numbing forty minutes after leaving the boardwalk. Melody ran up onto the porch, stomping her boots and shaking off the snow. She didn't know how she had managed to carry Maloos home. She pulled out the key with one hand, unlocked the door, pushed it open, and was greeted with a burst of warmth. Stumbling in, she set Maloos down. Both were exhausted, desperate for rest. She quickly shut the door behind her to keep the frigid air out and took off her boots. Removing Maloos's leash, she peeled off her frozen red coat, hanging it by the fireplace to dry. She then dried her wet little body with a towel and covered her with a patchwork quilt up to her neck as she laid down in her spot on the couch. Petting her head, she said, "I know you're cold. You sit here, I'll get a treat for you."

Maloos happily licked Melody's hand as she tucked the quilt under her. After her treat, she enjoyed a relaxing time snoozing on the couch under the big window in the living room.

Melody went upstairs, changed out of her wet clothes and into thick, warm pajamas. She returned to the living room. "Let's get that fire roaring and heat this place," she announced as she began piling logs on the andirons. Soon the fire was blazing. She stood beside the fireplace, warming first one side, then the other. Maloos napped with one eye open.

Warm at long last, she went to the kitchen and made a cup of hot cocoa. She settled herself in a chair close to the fire and wrapped her still-numb fingers around the warm cup. She took a sip and immediately felt its warmth spread through her body. She looked at the fire, the birch logs were piled high and crackled cheerfully. They threw their light on the soft color of the smooth walls, on which a few old paintings of hers hung. Outside light trickled in from the window above Maloos, for at four o'clock the day had not yet faded to twilight and the chintz covers of the sofa, the bright toned pattern of the Persian rug, and the leaping flames on the hearth made the room cheerful. Every utterance from the wind chimes outside created a soothing symphony in odd time. Maloos snored serenely while Melody sat silently gazing at the leaping, dancing fire. She envied Maloos's ability to shut out the world and sleep.

Her mind ran over the past few weeks, thinking of her mother and her burial: of all the years she spent with her. Her mouth grew sour as a lump formed in her throat and tears gathered in the corners of her eyes. For a few moments she tried in vain to restrain the flow of her tears. She thought about the cabin and how such a simple, small, quiet place had brought pleasure and fulfillment to her family for years. Things were different when Bella was younger: There weren't enough hours in the day to fit in all the fun and games they loved so much. She recalled cold winter nights when Bella and Virginia would put marshmallows on sticks and roast them to a golden brown in the fireplace flame. They would then eat them through messy, grinning mouths.

She thought of how her mom had done the same with her when she was a child. Those days had passed; they left her wading through her memories. She often felt frozen in time, unable to move on from the blissfulness she had felt as a child and before Bella had moved out.

Melody was not happy with the fast-moving world: Fast food, fast internet, fast cars, instant gratification, instant communication, always on, always connected to the anchor in your pocket, yet always distant from the one right next to you. Innumerable amounts of cable channels, tweets, notifications, updates, stories, pictures, a constant flow of nonsense that has no impact on one's life except for the fact that it takes you away from the here, the now, the present world that is so fragile, so delicate that the slightest amount of neglect throws everything out of balance. Puffed with pride and overflowing with baseless self-importance, humans deteriorate into apes grunting responses from behind glowing screens as they paint a fabricated picture of the life they want to show others they live.

She believed that all of this sabotaged the family and their time together. Everyone worked all the time and decompressed by streaming endless content, endless news feeds, endless movies and shows right into their brains. After Bella finished college, Melody expected her to move back home. When that didn't happen, Melody and Virginia would instead anticipate Bella's arrival to the cabin for whatever occasion. Eventually, Bella would bring along Jeff, then Maloos, and new memories were made. Yet Melody watched as devices became appendages; as checking and scrolling became second nature; as the once bustling house fell more and more silent. Now she was there, alone, listening to the dog snore.

She recalled the simplicity of the past, when her world seemed so small, beautiful, and different; when, on snowy days, they played games, baked cookies, curled up with mugs of hot chocolate as they listened to the wind howl, and enjoyed the lazy, content confinement that only winter and snow could bring. When her family was together in unity, even winter's worst couldn't disrupt their spirit.

What a different time, she thought, recalling nights when they popped corn on the stove and watched their favorite movies; nights when they played games in the cabin; when winning came second to who could make the others laugh harder; nights when rain falling on the roof sounded like music to their ears. Virginia would bake bread in the early morning, letting the aroma draw the family downstairs like magnets to the kitchen, where she passed out thick slabs of warm bread topped with butter and her homemade jam for breakfast.

At least we have these wholesome, precious memories, she silently reflected.

She was lost in time: it either went slowly, traipsing lovingly through the past, or violently pushing forward through to the here and now.

Feeling the need to calm her inward self, she got up, shed the blanket, grabbed the snow shovel that sat inside the small closet by the front door, and went outside. Snow wrapped the cabin like a cocoon, transforming her small world into a wonderland. The old butterfly chime continued singing, even though some of its strings were broken. She shoveled the front porch and driveway, but the snow quickly covered it over. Her weak muscles began to ache. With fingers stiff, her knees and feet aching, she told herself she should stop shoveling and go inside. Submitting to her body's demands, she came into the house and decided to rest a while. She put more wood on the fire and held her hands close to the flames. She turned on her favorite song, "Stand by Me," causing Maloos to finally stir in her sleep. She then stretched out by the fireplace. She felt warm and hypnotized as she listened to the lovely music, covering her eyes with her hand. Music soothed and relaxed her. Moved by the music, she uncovered her eyes, looked at Maloos and asked, "Would you like to dance?" Maloos looked at her sleepily, then closed her eyes again.

Melody got up and laid down on the couch under the big living room window. The wind had subsided; huge snowflakes drifted lazily down onto a 5-inch blanket of snow. She shut out the day and listened to the music while her mind whirled into the past. In the distant woods she spotted an intricate, snow-laden spider web. She forgot all about her grief for a moment.

A pair of chipmunks were tunneling through the large aspen tree behind the cabin, rustling the snow loudly. Maloos heard the noise and sat up, growling grumpily while still half shrouded in her quilt. The chipmunks were gone by the time Maloos peered out the window, but a strange looking rabbit bounded by, traipsing through the falling snow. Maloos studied the unfamiliar creature for a second before barking loudly. Melody closed the curtains and turned off the CD player. Maloos stopped barking and laid down again.

Melody appreciated the silence and solitude: she felt warm and cozy curled up beside Maloos. She placed her arm around Maloos and looked at her face, her eyes brightly lit, her mouth so grimly set. Melody thanked God for such a wonderful creature. How had she ever hesitated at the notion of her company? Her presence brought such comfort to a troubled world.

Grief crept in again, replaying her mother's final breath. To distract her negative thoughts, she sat up and reached for the manuscript she had been working on. Touching Maloos's head tenderly, she asked, "Maloos, do you want to hear my new story?" Maloos opened her eyes groggily and stretched out her legs. She then stared sleepily at Melody, waiting. Love for the delicate creature coursed through Melody as she began reading. After a few pages, she felt very tired. She covered her face with her manuscript, drifting off with Maloos next to her.

When she woke up it was the early evening, the snow had stopped, the sky had cleared, and the sun was already disappearing behind the mountains. Soon the darkness, and the still silence that accompanies it in the mountains, returned. Melody relished the holy hush of the evenings in the mountains. She put more wood on the fire then poked at the wood as Maloos observed her. She held her hands to the warmth of the fire. All the negative thoughts once again overflowed, leaving her sad and restless.

She craved a coffee but knew that the caffeine would make it hard to sleep, and that was the last thing she needed now. Everything around her seemed gloomy. She thought of her family and her mother not being with them anymore. She noticed being with Maloos took her mind off her sadness for a while. She gave her the new toy that Bella had given her. Maloos then stood there maniacally shaking her prize. Melody played with her, laughing and tugging the toy from Maloos's clenched teeth.

The rest of the night, Melody relaxed in the company of Maloos, listening to music while reading. Maloos enjoyed being read to, so Melody did so, reciting one of her children's stories aloud. Melody also read aloud more chapters from her latest unfinished novel. Concluding the latest chapter, she wondered whether she would have the strength or energy to complete the story; or if she would even be able to paint something soon.

The darkness grew into night and the chill grew with it. The fire crackled warmth and bellowed welcome, familiar scents. The moon cast its light across a tapestry of pristine white. Shadows from towering pines gave the landscape a haunted look. She called Bella, checking in and updating her on the day. Bella reminded her to eat something. In the living room, next to the raging fire, Melody ate a quick supper of soup and bread. Belly now full, her bones ached of exhaustion. She was long overdue for a full night of sleep. She forced herself upstairs to the bedroom. Maloos jumped on the bed, ready for even more sleep. Melody glanced out of the upstairs window next to the bed, amazed at how the backyard and ancient house behind them looked so tranquil covered in white and lit by lunar light.

She dressed Maloos in warm pajamas and then went to the bathroom. After washing her face and brushing her teeth, she crawled into bed. Maloos, as usual, cuddled next to her like a baby bear. Lying in bed, she picked up a book and began reading it. Maloos sat up and barked. Melody told her to be quiet. Maloos laid back down, letting out two soft grunts in protest.

After reading a few more pages, she glanced at the clock. *8:15*, she thought, *I need to sleep.* She turned off the light and counted her blessings. Cold, she pulled the comforter up around her ears. She closed her eyes, but haunted thoughts of the day her mother passed returned again; the past burst through. *Oh, dear mind,* she prayed, *please stop thinking so much, I need to sleep. I am so tired!*

Gazing out the window, her thoughts led her to when they had bought this cabin when Bella was so small; to the sanctuary of the imagination where, for a brief moment, she could slip through time's barrier and once again enjoy her life. Her eyes closed, she dove headfirst into the happiness of years past: Birthdays, holidays, summer nights, the first day of spring, a winter solstice, sledding down hills, walking along paths, reaching the crest where the lake suddenly becomes visible. All such cherished times withered away until she felt hopeless and alone. She tossed restlessly, thinking *I am drowning in an ocean of perplexity. Please God, either quiet the waves or lift me above them.*

Maloos kicked her and scoffed, fed up with the tornado of movement and far too lazy and warm to find another spot.

Melody decided to respect the dog's demand: *If I can't have any peace*, she thought, *why should I rob her of it?* Either the stillness, or the fact that she had relinquished control, finally helped her sleep.

Maloos's furious barking woke Melody up around 9 p.m. Maloos was sitting up, looking out the bedroom window. She always guarded her family zealously, but Melody didn't recognize the high-pitched bark; its pitch seemed unusual.

Surprised by a slight headache, Melody sat up, snatching a pair of old glasses from the bedside table. "Who's there?" she asked Maloos. Maloos sprang like lightning towards the open door, continuing to bark while descending the stairs.

Without pausing for slippers, Melody followed. Her feet slipped; she fell to her knees. A small pain shot through her, but she ignored it. She got up then continued to the living room. As her eyes had adjusted to the dimness, she saw Maloos pawing at the front door, growling. Maloos often barked if she thought animals or people were close. Melody would placate her by opening the door or window, letting her see that there was no threat.

She turned on the porch light and opened the door. Maloos watched. It had stopped snowing, but bursts of high wind swept across the mountain. Freezing air tore into the warm cabin. Desperate to keep warm, Melody quickly scanned the walkway and yard, searching for signs of intruders or animals: a footprint, a shadow. Nothing. Horror eased away from her heart.

She snapped the door closed and turned towards Maloos. "See," she lovingly scolded, "nothing's out there. Now let's go to bed."

Maloos's eyes widened, staring intently at Melody. Following Melody into the living room, Maloos barked incessantly. Melody opened the curtains to the large window. The moonlight showered splendor across the backyard, illuminating a thick padding of fresh, sparkling snow. There were no signs of an intruder, animal or otherwise. Maloos ran back down the short hallway to the front door, barking so hard that her little body shook. Melody flipped on the living room light and stared at Maloos. Thinking she might need to go out to relieve herself, Melody donned her jacket and boots. After dressing Maloos, she attached her leash, turned on the porch lights again, and grasped the door handle.

Maloos gave a mysterious look as Melody opened the front door. She directed her attention back to Maloos, leading her out a few feet onto the front yard. "Come on,

Maloos," she coaxed. "Let's go potty."

It was a bitterly cold night. The snowy crust was

sheer ice now. Maloos stood for a few seconds in the cold

starlight, as if she was scared to take another step. She took

her time circling. "Please, Maloos," Melody begged

through chattering teeth, "please go! I am freezing!"

Maloos paused, looked at her intently, and barked.

She turned away from the yard and started pulling towards

the car. Puzzled, and getting annoyed, Melody planted

herself. The two struggled, the leash taut between them:

one pulling towards the house, the other towards the car.

Eventually, Melody won. She dragged Maloos in,

disregarded the wide-eyed, intense glare as typical stubborn

behavior. She closed the door sharply. She took off her

boots and jacket then extinguished the outside light.

Melody detached Maloos's leash. Free, she ran towards the

back door, barking all the way: Something had set off the

sensor lights in the backyard. Her heart racing, Melody opened the door slowly and looked out from behind the screen door. She became startled when her eyes met a raccoon's. Fear waning, she closed the door as Maloos continued barking furiously. Frustrated, Melody turned off the lights, picked up Maloos mid bark, causing the dog to let out air like a deflating tire, and carried her upstairs to bed.

"There you go," she said, laying her down gently. Just as Melody laid down, Maloos popped up and began barking irately, all the while looking intensely at Melody. Melody let out a sigh of frustration as Maloos took off across the room, running downstairs again, her ID tag jingling loudly as it clanged against its metal ring.

Melody was surprised: she had never seen Maloos act this way. Her headache seemed to be getting worse; a wave of exhaustion swallowed her. She thought that maybe Maloos had lost her sense of time from the long drive up;

that maybe all the sleeping she had done that day had screwed up her internal clock. Her eyes wide, she let out another deep sigh, releasing the frustration that swelled insider her.

"Maloos!" she called, her voiced riddled with annoyance. "Maloos!" she repeated louder.

Maloos continued barking.

"Maloos," she called, "Come back to bed!"

Maloos barked and barked but didn't return.

Melody slapped her open hand against the covers. "Oh, God, what is *wrong* with you?" as Maloos continued throwing her shrill fit.

She lay for a few minutes, hoping Maloos would get over her tantrum. The barking continued. Melody got up, went to the top of the stairs and called, "Maloos! Maloos! Come up here! Come on! Please!"

Maloos ignored her and continued barking her short, percussive barks. No amount of calling coaxed her upstairs.

Melody went down a few steps then paused. Noting Maloos's upturned face, Melody asked, "Do you want a treat?"

She didn't. Bribery had never before failed with Maloos. Desperate, Melody started meowing, whistling, even stamping her foot. All the odd noises that usually got Maloos's attention failed. She kept screaming out her increasingly annoying barks. Maloos wouldn't budge. She simply paced back and forth by the front door, tossing her head back and shrieking herself hoarse.

"What is going on?" Melody whispered, her fatigue and headache expanding. The little creature that normally followed behind her, that slept so soundly beside her, that inerrantly answered to the promise of treats, was being wholly unruly. Melody kept calling from the stairs.

Finally, Melody went down. Maloos was pacing by the front door, her tail tucked between her legs, her body jolting with each utterance she let fly.

"Maloos, what's wrong?" Melody asked gently, growing concerned.

Her eyes wide with fright, Maloos stared at her. She then sat on her hind legs and cocked her head to one side. The two stared at each other silently.

Unable to understand whatever message Maloos was trying to communicate, Melody broke the silence. "Come on, Maloos," she impatiently commanded. "Let's go back to bed!"

Maloos looked at her silently. The pupils in her eyes seemed to grow. She let slip the bark of dog.

Melody recalled her daughter's words in almost a mocking tone: "Maloos is a great source of entertainment, and not much of a bother." She burst out laughing. Gazing upwards at her with fiery eyes, Maloos fumed. In a thunderous voice, she let Melody know how incensed she was.

Melody raised her eyebrows, astonished at the tiny beast's challenge. She sat down beside Maloos, placed a hand on her back, and tried to calm her. "Maloos," she said silently, "I want you to stop."

But Maloos turned away and kept barking. "Stop!" Melody shouted, stunning herself. Regardless, Maloos ignored her.

Anger boiled inside Melody. She shut her eyes and plugged her ears. *I made a serious mistake bringing her here*, she thought. The anger waned. She opened her eyes and unplugged her ears. She placed her hand on Maloos's back again and petted her softly. "Listen," she said firmly over Maloos's barks, "you must not bark. You have to be quiet. I am very tired and want to go to bed." She then stood up slowly and motioned for Maloos to come.

Yapping, Maloos bolted into the living room and jumped on the sofa. Melody chased her, arms open in attempt to swoop her up. Maloos predicted Melody's movements, jumped off the sofa, and climbed on to the other couch. They danced chaotically until Melody tried to chase Maloos upstairs. Maloos predicted this too and side-stepped Melody so quickly that Melody almost fell.

"Maloos!" Melody boomed. "SIT DOWN!"

Maloos bowed and snapped out another series of high-pitched barks that cracked like lightening.

"Fine!" Melody yelled. Her headache now screaming, turned and began climbing upstairs as Maloos kept yapping. "You bark as long as you want! I'm going to bed!"

Melody soon laid on the bed. She covered her face with both hands. She was mad at herself for bringing Maloos. *Never again*, she thought angrily, fantasizing of telling her daughter just how bad of a dog Maloos had been. Maloos continued disturbing the peace below.

Melody went downstairs again to find Maloos still standing by the front door, chirping away. Once again, Maloos ran to the living room as Melody approached her.

"MALOOS! COME HERE RIGHT NOW!" she shouted.

Maloos stopped barking and stared at her, then took off, running laps around the living room, through the hallway, and to the front door. Melody ran after her as best as her knees would let her. Just when she finally thought she had bested the dog, a quick turn landed her flat on her back.

Melody whimpered from pain and frustration. She stood up and went to fetch the biggest, juiciest morsel of a treat she could find from Maloos's bag. In her most singsong, promising voice, she asked, "Do you want a treaty treat?"

Maloos stopped in her tracks. She looked at Melody, the treat, then back at Melody and barked.

Melody threw the treat back into the bag and chased

Maloos through the living room, around the dining table,

over the sofa, into the kitchen and back out again, all the

while yelling at her to stop. But she didn't. After what

seemed to be the hundredth lap, Melody felt an

overwhelming sense of the absurdity. She stopped chasing

and doubled over laughing.

Maloos stopped running as well and barked

furiously. Melody sprang forward, surprising Maloos, who

ran backwards into the living room, through the short

hallway, and to the front door. She was finally cornered.

She barked, making it clear that the standoff would not end

peacefully.

Melody's face glowed red, contorted with rage and

disappointment, the laughter she let out a short while ago

now lost in the melee. She finally exploded. "YOU ARE A

BAD GIRL! SIT DOWN!"

Maloos stopped barking and sat down. Melody snatched her up, determined to carry her up to the bedroom where she would shut the door and keep them both locked in until morning. She held her tightly, as the little creature wiggled and whipped in vain attempts to break free again. Melody carried her upstairs and into the bedroom. She shut the door with an angry bang.

Melody lay Maloos on the bed. Maloos flattened out her front paws and placed her muzzle down. Her eyes roaming, a sharp sigh signaled her frustration, all the while her tail swayed as rhythmically as a metronome.

"Okay," Melody said definitively, "enough playing around. Time to sleep. Now."

Laying back on her pillow, Melody closed her eyes. She wondered if Maloos could understand how desperately she needed sleep and if she would succumb to Melody's demands.

Maloos stayed for a moment, her tail slapping against the covers. She shifted to one side and laid still. She shifted to the other side and laid still again. She shifted once more, causing Melody to lightly nudge her with her knee. Maloos sprang up, standing on all fours and shattered the silence yet again.

Melody jolted up, perplexed by the newly high-strung dog. She knew dogs used their eyes and body language to communicate, but she couldn't understand what she was trying to tell her. Her annoyance fell away; Now she was beginning to worry. *Was someone outside the cabin, in the backyard?*

"Maloos," she asked softly, "what's wrong?" Maloos looked at her.

She rose from bed and peered out the window to their fenced backyard. The light from the patio shone out onto unmarred snow. The moonlight revealed no trespasser, not even a prowling critter. She picked up Maloos and guided her vision to the outside, showing her everything she had just examined. "See, Maloos," she said as the dog's chest reverberated with muted growls, "nothing. There aren't any animals. Nobody is outside. Everything is fine and perfect." She ran her fingers through Maloos's curly hair, "Let's go back to sleep now," she cooed. Maloos growled. "Please, I am very exhausted." Maloos looked at her with a sad, almost blank stare. She squirmed to get closer to Melody and licked her face, her large, round eyes, full of an unreadable expression.

Melody put her on the bed and wormed under the warm covers, resting her heavy head on her pillow. Maloos had finally stopped barking. She sat on the bed looking out the window. With a deep sigh, she then lay down, nestled in Melody's arms. Melody looked at the clock, *9:55!* she thought incredulously. *You kept up this charade for almost an entire hour!* She let out a small chuckle at the stubborn dog, then closed her eyes.

The silence inside the room was shattered again by Maloos's barking. Melody sprang up. Her head was killing her. She felt severely nauseous. The clock read 10:17 p.m. Melody threw her head back onto the pillow, her eyes heavy. Maloos crawled towards Melody, her tail wagging furiously. She barked and licked her face non-stop. Melody tried to push her away but Maloos leaned in with force and continued licking, as if to keep her from sleeping. Melody sat up again, her headache splitting, her eyes heavy from fatigue. Maloos put her paws on Melody's chest then barked as loud as she could. It made no sense.

"BE QUIET!" Melody shouted. Maloos barked louder, pushing against her chest with force.

Melody let out a scream of frustration and threw her head against the pillow once more. Maloos now stood on her chest, her face looking down into Melody's. "Up! Up!" she seemed to say with absurd force.

Melody lay astonished, thinking that Maloos had lost her mind. To the contrary, Maloos was alert, strong, and determined. "STOP IT!" Melody screamed, goaded into rage by her own confusion.

Maloos stopped barking and fell silent. She loomed over Melody, her eyes staring into hers. The pressure from Maloos standing on her chest took her mind off of her headache and her eyes began to close. Maloos growled and the let out a high-pitched yelp.

"Ok!" she said, sitting up and throwing the blanket off of her. "Make me suffer, go on," she mumbled, swing her legs to the side of the bed. "I'll never bring you here again!"

She looked at Maloos, who sat on the bed, staring right back.

"What's *wrong* with you?" Melody asked. "Are you sick? Why are you barking? You must be sick. You don't look well, and you don't sound well." Melody remembered her daughter said that a dog's gums can indicate if they are healthy or sick: if pale, they are sick, if pink, the dog is healthy. Melody turned on the bedside lamp then reached out to pull Maloos's bottom lip, but the dog was far too quick. Maloos jumped out of bed and bounded to the bedroom door, her collar clanging furiously, all the while barking.

"GET TO BED!" she shouted. "NOW!" Maloos barked back, the two of them trapped in a call and response of command and refusal.

"Bark as much as you like," she shouted angrily. "I'll sleep!"

She felt ridiculous. She pulled the comforter up and over her head as Maloos began pawing at the bedroom door and growling. The scratching was disturbing, but the chamber she created in which she lay provided a level of warmth and solace that made the noise seem distant. Her head ached and she felt queasy again. *Lack of sleep always makes me ill*, she thought as her breathing became more rhythmic and her eyelids started to close.

Maloos jumped onto the bed, worked her way under the cover, and stared into Melody's face. She licked her face furiously, nudging her with her nose between each lick. Melody sat up, tossing the comforter off. A rush of chilly air shocked her out of her grogginess. Maloos jumped off the bed, ran to the door once more, sat, and stared at Melody. Melody sat silently in bed, looking out the bedroom window, ignoring the demander in the room. Maloos let out a low growl that changed octaves to a high-pitched bark, all in one long breath.

Melody rose, walked to Maloos, knelt down and petted her head gently. "What's wrong, Maloos?" she asked, her voice hoarse

Maloos looked at her, the slivers of the whites in her eyes made them appear larger. Her furry mouth formed an "o" as she let out a low, muted growl. Melody touched her nose, causing Maloos to pause. *Cold and wet*, Melody thought. *Normal.* Maloos leaned back on the hind legs she sat on, raised her paws high, and scratched at the air.

Melody took this as a sign that Maloos wanted to be picked up, so she obliged. Holding the dog close to her chest, she went to the bedroom window, and whispered, "Look Maloos, look!" Maloos directed her attention to the window. Whether she was entranced by the reflection of the two, or by something far off in the white wonderland beyond, Melody could not tell. She bounced Maloos lightly as if she were an infant. "See? Nothing! Everything is fine." Maloos started her low growl again.

They stood at the large window, Melody's gaze slowly roaming over the woods, ignoring the old house behind them. Her eyes were searching again for any signs of an intruder or animal. Usually winter offered an empty and desolate view from her cabin. That night, however, the full moon made the snow look like a vast ocean of diamonds. The icicles caught the moonlight almost like a prism, transforming the bright light into a frosted glow deep within the chest of each dangling pick. Entranced, as if the beauty built up her courage, she allowed her eyes to wander to the old house behind her cabin. Suddenly, the house was the scariest it had ever been.

Algol

Corralled behind a dilapidated fence, thin, necrotic apple trees stabbed up from the ground as if awakened by a curse. Lonely and neglected, bowing from their robes of white. An ancient bristlecone pine clung to the wall of the old cabin; its creeping branches framed the entrance to the house, cannibalistically consuming rotted siding. The old tree had shaded the cabin from a hot sun in the summer and held off raging wind and snow in the winter. Now, its vast shadow blocked out the moonlight, obscuring an aspen tree behind it. A twisted, crumbling chimney spanned the entire length of one side of the house, the shadows giving the illusion it had separated entirely from the wall. Peeling red paint exposed dark, decaying wood. A broken window decorated the second floor. An old, green awning above the window had crumbled under the weight of a snowstorm over a decade ago. The cloth flapped uselessly in the wind.

Melody was reminded of a heavyweight boxer's bruised, broken, and bloodied face.

Residents around the old cabin had heard stories from their neighbors, perhaps in passing while on a walk, perhaps having been sought out after moving in. Either way, the stories always began the same: an old man had told someone who had told them and now they were telling you. The first story starred a young woman of about 20, whose uneasy spirit escapes every full moon from the wall in which she was sealed up alive by her captor: a deranged squatter taking advantage of the low population in the mountain city during the early 1940's. The woman, true to the restlessness of her now permanent age (or, of course, the circumstances of her death), moved about the silent rooms searching for her murderer: a ceaselessly futile hunt in which you, the innocent warm body, want to avoid being collateral damage.

The second story told of a bride abandoned at the alter by her philandering fiancé. Seeking solace from the humiliation of being discarded, she fled to a familiar cabin she had frequented in her youth. She ended up swinging from the second story banister, an extension cord wrapped around her neck. The whites of her wide eyes dyed red, she swayed listlessly for four days in a flowing, ornately embroidered, sequined white dress, a pearl tiara accenting braided hair that framed a mascara streaked face with a clown-like frown. Pinned to her was a note of two words, her last contribution to the collective conscious: "Leave me?!" it read antagonistically.

Another story told of piano music that could be heard coming from the broken upstairs window, even though no piano was in the house. Yet another storyteller would have you believe a white apparition constantly floats up and down the stairs. Others combined two fables, warning that, if you looked hard enough, for long enough, on just the right night, the ghosts of the murdered woman and the would-be-wife could be seen behind the dusty old windows. Others said they could hear the sound of an ax splitting wood, followed by the bang of the porch door as the wood was carried into the house. Then the stove door squeaked as it opened, followed by the rustling of coals before wood was piled on top and the door slammed shut.

Having owned their cabin for three decades, Melody had heard just about every fantastical murmur about the house that the locals could drum up. Some regaled the stories with amusement, while others gave the house a wide berth. Those who had the courage to investigate never saw anyone or heard anything. Nevertheless, nearing the house could give an eerie feeling to the easily influenced. *Everything you can imagine is real*, Melody would often think as she looked at the house, a sense of wonder overtaking her as she pondered the stories and the stories behind them.

When Melody and her husband first bought their cabin, they had no knowledge of the rumors circulating the house behind them. Owning it for so many years, she never bothered to probe deeper and ask who, exactly, had witnessed the supernatural happenings firsthand. Deep down, she knew they were urban legends meant to add a little excitement to the mundane mountain life.

Despite being a rational skeptic, Maloos's behavior left her feeling unsure. *What if the stories were true?* she thought. *What if some 95-year-old mountain man actually was sending a warning by word of mouth to everyone in the community?* Uneasiness turned into fear that Maloos might have seen a ghost.

A cold, piercing panic impaled her: an icicle straight through her heart and into her spine. She let out a long breath as Maloos growled on. The abandoned house behind their cabin remained still and quiet, the supposed ghosts inside unaffected by the storm of barking and yelling coming from their inconsiderate neighbors.

Melody forced her mind to grip onto reality, reminding herself that ghosts were the product of an overactive conscience or imagination. When they were young, she had told Bella to "sweep away cobwebs of superstition that ignorance and fear have ever been weaving around inside your minds."

"I needn't worry," she told herself aloud, peeling her gaze from the weak, old structure outside.

Maloos stared at Melody, her chest still vibrating from her guttural growling, her large eyes full of apprehension. Feeling overtired, Melody put Maloos down on the bed and sat down next to her. "Come on," she told Maloos who stood on the comforter, "let's go to bed now."

Melody reached to turn off the bedside lamp and Maloos burst out of the bed, kicking the blankets back with such force that they bunched up into little waves on the bed.

Her bark filled the room as she made her way to the door yet again, pacing back and forth.

Melody's body tensed; she hunched her shoulders, squinted her eyes, and held her hands in tight fists. "Come to bed," she said through clenched, grinding teeth.

Maloos paced defiantly, her hoarse voice echoing a cry of fear. Melody saw that her tail was tucked between her legs.

What is she afraid of? Melody thought. *What if she has seen a ghost?* The absurdity of the thought was waved away by her own hand.

Melody ignored her now throbbing headache, got up, and sat down beside Maloos. Maloos's eyes roamed about the room chaotically. "Sit," she commanded Maloos, who obliged. "Focus," she said, holding her index finger to the tip of her nose. Maloos's eyes trained upon the point of Melody's nose. Melody had her attention. The room was so silent that Melody could hear her own heartbeat. As she sat there, frozen in place by her own imagination, she knew she had to solve the mystery of Maloos's constant barking.

Exhausted, worried, and terrified, she sat facing Maloos. Imagine what she would tell me if she could only talk, she thought.

"Do you want some water?" she asked, standing up to fetch the water cup by the side of the bed.

Maloos stood on all fours and started barking yet again.

"Ugh!" Melody cried out. "Please stop! PLEASE!"

Maloos barked louder, the high register echoing through the room like a fire alarm.

"STOP IT!" Melody yelled, snapping her fingers.

Maloos avoided looking at her and pitched her voice louder.

"DO YOU HEAR WHAT I AM SAYING? STOP IT! NO BARKING!" She pointed her finger at her and shouted furiously, "KEEP IT DOWN!"

Maloos didn't seem to care at all, her focus trained on making as much noise as possible.

Desperate for help, Melody thought that maybe she should call someone. *Both her daughter and husband wouldn't be much help*, she thought, *it was too late, and they were too far. Besides*, she thought, *calling them at this time of night would spark panic in them and they would immediately come up the mountain no matter how much I protest*. She felt comforted knowing she could rely on them if need be.

She thought of the local animal society, after all, they had a small zoo showcasing the regional species and experts to care for them. *Surely someone would be able to offer insight on an unruly dog*. The idea fell immediately away when she realized that they were closed. *The local veterinarian would be closed too*, she thought. *As was the pet store and the groomer*.

Maloos growled and began barking again.

The only option, she thought with embarrassment, *is the police*. She hated the idea of calling them over something that is in no way an emergency, but she was clueless. She stood up, went to the bedside table where her cellphone lay, and found the police station number in her contacts. Her hand trembled as she put the phone up to her ear.

Exodus

The call was picked up midway through the third ring. "Hello," Melody said anxiously. Maloos stopped barking and stared at Melody.

"Sheriff's station," answered a woman on the other end of the line. "How can I help you?"

"Hi, sorry," Melody replied, her voice quivering slightly, "I'm having trouble with my dog and have no idea who to call." Though she felt embarrassed, she knew that there was hardly any excitement in the mountain community and that the local sheriff and their crew were bored most of the time.

"Ok," the woman responded, slightly intrigued. "What is going on with your dog?

"Well, she seemed fine when we got here earlier today," Melody explained. "We went on a walk, then she slept for a while, ate dinner, relieved herself and everything.

But for the last hour or so she has been barking nonstop!" Melody looked at Maloos, who silently stared back.

"Perhaps she heard something outside?" the woman asked.

"I checked," Melody responded confidently. "There is nothing: no animals, no people, not even footprints in the snow."

"Maybe she's sick?" the dispatcher asked. "Her gums should be a healthy pink; can you check them for me right now?"

"I tried earlier but she wouldn't let me," Melody replied. "Let me try again." She reached forward with her finger outstretched. Maloos let her lift her lips and examine her gums. "Yep, they are fine," Melody said touching Maloos's nose. "Physically she seems fine to me."

There was a short pause. "Maybe," the woman began inquisitively, "maybe she smells something like gas or carbon monoxide. Is your home equipped with a carbon monoxide detector?"

"Yes," Melody answered. "I always plug in the batteries when we arrive…" Like a flash, it occurred to her that she had forgotten all about the carbon monoxide detector. "But," she began again slowly, "I forgot to."

"I'll stay on the line while you go ahead and turn it on," the woman said calmly.

"Ok," Melody said. Holding her cell phone, she opened the door, exited the room, and hurried down the steps. Maloos followed her. The alarm and the battery were on a table near the sofa. She placed her cell phone on the table, then put the battery in carbon monoxide detector. The little device started squealing almost immediately. The high-pitched beeping shocked Melody, causing her heart to skip a beat. In that moment everything made sense: Maloos wanted to leave the house. She wouldn't let Melody sleep. She even tried to get her out of bed by force.

Melody picked up her cell phone. "Oh, my gosh! You're right! It is carbon monoxide!"

"Ma'am," the woman said sternly, "everyone at the residence must exit immediately, pets included. Don't wait. We will send the fire department. Wait outside until they arrive."

"We're leaving," Melody said. She thanked her and hung up the phone. She was relieved that Maloos wasn't barking because of an intruder or some perceived ghost. However, she was terrified that they'd both been breathing poison.

She hurried to the bedroom and changed into clothes, only half aware of what she was putting on. Maloos followed her everywhere, watching her every move without barking. She turned to Maloos and said lovingly, "Quick! Maloos! We have to leave! Now!"

Rushing down the stairs with Maloos trailing zigzag behind her, she nearly jumped into her snow boots, pulled on a pair of warm gloves, pocketed her phone, and wrapped Maloos in a thick, fleece lined blanket. She picked up Maloos with one hand, stored her keys in another pocket after unlocking her car, and opened the front door. The clean, crisp air was almost shocking to her: the stale air in the cabin seemed to hang like a dense cloud in her mind. The outside air washed away the muck, allowing her to feel like a newborn taking its first breath. She inhaled deeply as she ran toward her car, now cradling Maloos in both arms. Icy snow crunched under her feet and she took effort not to slip and fall. The pine trees, pathway, and parking lot were frosted like a wedding cake. The tip of her nose and ears felt frosty as she rushed away from the open cabin door.

Maloos watched with approval as she opened the car door. She placed Maloos in the front passenger seat. "I'm so sorry I shouted at you," she apologized as she leaned over the driver's seat, her fingers lovingly combing through Maloos's thick, curly hair. "You are a little lifesaver! I am so proud of you!"

Maloos beamed, licking her lips and letting Melody apologize. Melody closed the passenger door and went to the other side of the car. She fetched a blanket from the rear, then opened the driver's side door. She turned on the car and cranked the heater. Frosty air blew out of the vents, but she knew it warm up soon. Melody then covered Maloos with the blanket from the back of her car and said, "Stay here Maloos. I'll be back in a minute."

Covered and warm, Maloos plopped down in the seat, laying her head on the seat's armrest. She didn't defy Melody and try to follow her as she closed the door and hurriedly ran back into the house.

Inside, Melody threw open all the windows downstairs then up. She ran back down, grabbed a heavy quilt from the couch in the living room, shoved a bag of treats from the dining room table into her coat pocket, and carefully hurried back to her car. Inside, she waited for the firemen to arrive. The cabin began to get warm, and fearing another Carbon Monoxide leak, Melody turned off the car. Maloos's eyes seemed to grow heavy as Melody covered herself with the quilt.

"The firemen are on their way," Melody said with a sigh of relief.

Maloos turned to her and gave her a wondering look. Melody took a treat from her pocket and gave it to Maloos. Down it went with gulping relish. After hugging her again, she told her what a wonderful thing she'd done and that she was so sorry that she'd yelled.

Maloos understood the apologetic tones and actions and kindly looked up at Melody with soft brilliance as if telling her, "You should always listen to me rather than point your finger and yell." The little angel laid her head down onto the seat and was soon fast asleep.

As she sat in silence inside the car, Melody looked out the window, past some melted snow, and saw millions of stars high overhead. She was far less frustrated and enjoyed the crowds of stars looking upon her, glittering and winking in the dark. She realized that her headache was fading, as well as her nausea.

Melody waited in the freezing car with her companion. The distant sound of coyotes howling in the woods didn't even stir an exhausted Maloos. Melody looked at her, thinking: *This creature suffered and tolerated all my nasty shouting and wickedness to show that she loved me!* She recalled something her mother always said: "The people who do things for you are the ones who really love you. If they say they have love for you, but do not reach out to you, their words are hollow and ingenuine."

After about ten minutes, the firemen pulled silently into the driveway, their red lights lighting up the neighborhood like a flashing Christmas tree. Awakened, Maloos stood up and looked out the window. She barked hoarsely.

"Shhh," Melody said quietly, petting Maloos's head softly. "They are here to help us." Maloos looked at her curiously.

Melody got out of her car carrying a blanket wrapped Maloos in her arms. Her feet slid out from under her, and both she and Maloos plopped down on the slippery driveway. She got up, laughing over her clumsiness. *We always seem so helpless when rescue workers arrive*, she thought. She walked toward the fire truck.

Two firemen stepped out and one asked if she had called about a carbon monoxide leak. She pulled Maloos closer to her chest and said, "Yes, I called."

Upon meeting the firemen, Maloos began furiously wagging her tail as if she knew they had come to rescue them. She leaned out of Melody's arms, desperate to lick the unfamiliar faces. The firemen stepped closer, granting Maloos her wish and patting her on the head.

"How did you notice a carbon monoxide leak was in your home?" asked the younger of the two.

"I put a battery in the detector and it immediately went off," she started. "But before that, my dog woke me up with incessant barking," she laughed. "I was so annoyed and confused!"

The older fireman smiled and said, "Dogs are quick to warn their owners of danger."

They all went inside the cabin. The older of the two pulled out a carbon monoxide detector and turned it on. The reading showed that the level of carbon monoxide inside the house was 150 parts per million. The older fireman explained that if they had spent any more time inside the house, they easily could have died.

"This level of carbon monoxide exposure," he explained, "causes headaches, fatigue, and nausea. Carbon monoxide accumulates in the blood stream, attaching to hemoglobin and displacing oxygen. Essentially, your tissue and cells begin decaying from lack of oxygen. For levels up to 101 parts per million, you must ventilate and evacuate your home for at least two hours as there is a still a high risk for carbon poisoning. However, it doesn't seem as if you were exposed for long, probably just around the time your dog started barking."

"But I didn't smell any gas or anything!" Melody said.

"The gas is odorless and colorless," the younger fireman chimed in. "So, it's important to have a properly functioning carbon monoxide detector on at all times."

"That's so scary!" Melody said. "If it wasn't for my dog's constant barking, I would be dead before dawn!"

"Absolutely," the older one replied. "Carbon monoxide and gas leaks are the most common hazards that animal owners have been made aware of by their four-legged friends. And that's because CO2 often affects dogs and cats first, causing them to act erratically. We've seen many incidents like this in the mountains."

He then patted Maloos on the head and said, "She barked because she sensed that you both were in danger. She saved you."

Joyfully, Melody kissed Maloos's head and said with great pride, "Yes! She is my angel, my life saver! From now on whenever she barks it will certainly be music to my ears instead of a nuisance." Despite being exhausted from too much barking and lack of sleep, Maloos relished in the attention and praise.

After making sure all gas appliances inside the cabin were off, the younger fireman went outside and shut off the gas supply at the meter control valve. The other checked the fireplace and noticed that the soot had built up in the chimney. He directed Melody's attention to the fireplace and said, "It is essential to make sure your flue is open all the way at all times and that you have a professional come out to clean the chimney regularly. An open, clean passage allows the carbon monoxide from the fireplace to rise and dissipate. The blockage here and the wood you burned earlier could be a recipe for danger."

Melody nodded, embarrassed. "I will make sure to get it looked at immediately."

"It happens," the fireman replied. "As a safety measure, the best way to protect your family is to ensure you have a working carbon monoxide alarm in your home all the time. That way the alarm will sound, and you can all leave safely."

He then urged her to call the gas company first thing in the morning and let them know she had a suspected carbon monoxide leak. In the midst of all this, Melody found out just how lucky she was to have Maloos with her on this trip. Clutching Maloos tight to her chest, the fireman said, "This little dog is your guardian angel!"

Upon the firemen's departure, Melody decided that she and Maloos would sleep in the car for a few hours. She closed the door to the cabin to prevent any critters from entering and walked to her car. She was not excited over the thought of sleeping in a freezing car, but she had no choice: the cabin was off-limits and leaving the mountain so late at night was dangerous. She didn't even have chains on her tires. There were plenty of hotels in the mountain, but she doubted any of them would be open. She resigned herself to bundling both of them up as best she could in the thick blankets she'd gathered earlier.

Inside the car, she covered Maloos. Exhausted, the dog collapsed and went to sleep right away. Melody finally slept just after midnight, falling victim to the sudden fatigue that follows an adrenaline rush. She awoke just before 4 a.m. and went into the house, shivering. The cabin was cold, but the reading from the carbon monoxide detector showed that everything was normal. She closed all of the windows and went outside to fetch Maloos.

Inside again, they trudged upstairs where Maloos jumped onto a very welcoming bed. Melody turned on two heating pads and put them under the comforter. As Melody was getting into her pajamas, Maloos circled a few times and found warm spot over the heating pad on the bed and laid down.

After giving Maloos a big hug, she went to bed thinking: *This little, dependent creature showed me incomparable love, saved me from dying, and gave me a second chance to live my life.* She kissed her and told her, "I love you Maloos. I shall forever remember this night and you for the wonderful thing you did for me. Your persistence, courage, and sturdiness kept me alive."

With an overwhelming sense of comfort, Melody finally went into a deep sleep.

She woke up late the next morning, the sun brightening a light-blue sky, indicating new hope on her horizon. Snow sparkled on the treetops and branches outside her window. She laid in bed let out a deep sigh of contentment. *If it wasn't for Maloos waking me up last night*, she thought, *I would never have met this new day*. The sun broke through the mountain pines as Melody gathered Maloos in her arms and covered her face with kisses.

Maloos licked her face with her warm tongue and took the time to greet her in bed and brighten her day. Both of them stayed in their warm bed another thirty more minutes before finally rising.

Standing at the window, she opened her mind and soul to the beauty around her, allowing her heart to fill with how wonderous life was. She thanked Maloos again, thinking: *Nothing is constant except change.* She acknowledged that death is a part of life, and that everyone experienced it at some point and still managed to glue their broken hearts back together and push forward.

"I cannot let my grief pause my existence anymore; I must always move, either toward the front or toward the rear. But if I move forward, I must have ideals; the worthiest ideals are always revealed through the vision of the soul."

Her mind again was rejoicing over everything that had happened the night before: the realization of life caused the murky waters of sadness and pain to be diluted with hope of a new future before her. How supremely interesting it would be to watch the development of everything as that future unfolded in its richness and glory. The thought of it all was sweet indeed.

Grief may not vanish entirely, she thought, *but that's life, and put in their proper perspective, maybe they can be more easily understood.*

She had often heard the theory that dogs lived in the "now" but had finally understood it through Maloos. She knew that she herself was the opposite: that she had been influenced or controlled by almost every circumstance.

Gazing at Maloos's face resting so peacefully on the bed, as if nothing had happened a few short hours before, she thought: *Living in the now with our face toward the future and back toward the past is the secret of her content life! Let the past slip behind you, the Now will always be here, you can never escape it. Then why fight the Universal Law of Change? Why would I want a life that has grown stale? Change is the only thing that makes life worth living. To Maloos, change means life!*

Why not welcome each day as a new day fresh from the mint of the universe, as Maloos does? Why not bid each day goodbye when we retire for the night, saying: "Farewell, old day; you have served well your purpose; go your way in peace, leaving me to enter into life the countless days to follow in which I will live and move and

rejoice my being."

She decided to be more determined like Maloos; to have more faith in herself; to be stronger and more positive.

Elated, she packed up their things. She closed up the cabin, making sure everything was in its place. As she shut and locked the cabin door, she saw the old butterfly chime hanging on front porch. Even though some of its strings were loose or broken, the old chime sat dangling at an angle, making sweet music. She realized how that chime was just like her heart: Years of wind, rain, snow, and heat had damaged and altered it. However, it was still a chime, still functional, still singing a beautifully unique song that danced on the wind and disappeared into the hearts of whomever heard it.

She buckled Maloos into the car, planting a kiss on her furry forehead, astounded at the pure and simple love such a small creature could show. She got into the car, stared out of the window and formed a silent wish: that

peace would spread its blessing like light and guide her life

through the night.

Acknowledgments

Many thanks to Phillip Villarreal for editing this book.

Thanks to my exceptional friend, Susan Walker for her
support and encouragement.

www.ingramcontent.com/pod-product-compliance
Lightning Source LLC
Chambersburg PA
CBHW060639130626
46555CB00002B/876

* 9 7 8 0 5 7 8 8 0 6 7 1 6 *